RAJ MARAWAR

THE DRAGONS REVENGE

The legend of a brave warrior

Part 1

TO MY FAMILY

Content:

The Invasion Begins

The sky was never supposed to look like that.

A sickly green glow stretched across the heavens, twisting the clouds into unnatural shapes. Elowen had read stories about the end of the world before, but none of them had prepared her for what she saw now.

The invasion had begun.

It started with a deep, bone-rattling hum that rolled through the town like a distant storm. Then, the ships appeared. They were enormous, dark, and nothing like the sleek flying saucers from movies. These were jagged and mechanical, their exteriors shifting like living metal. As they flew over the city, beams of searing white light shot down, turning entire buildings to dust in seconds.

Elowen stood frozen in the middle of the street, her heart pounding against her ribs. She had always imagined herself as someone who would fight, someone brave. But now, standing before the terrifying display of power, all she could do was watch.

A group of people sprinted past her, their screams cutting through the air. A father yanked his crying daughter along as debris rained down around them. An elderly woman collapsed, her shaking hands clutching her chest as she struggled to move. The air smelled of burning metal and something else—something acrid and wrong.

"Elowen! Get inside!" her mother's voice snapped her out of her trance. She turned, her mother's face pale and drawn with fear. "Now!"

Elowen bolted toward their house, stumbling up the front steps. Her father was already at the window, pulling the curtains shut, his hands trembling. Outside, the streets were a mess of overturned cars, shattered glass, and fallen streetlights. The aliens had only just arrived, and yet, the town was already unrecognizable.

She dropped to the floor, trying to catch her breath. Her hands were shaking. She wanted to believe this was some awful nightmare, but the screams outside made it impossible.

Elowen had always been fascinated by dragons—powerful, untamed creatures that ruled the skies in myths and legends. She had spent countless nights sketching them, imagining what it would be like if they were real. But as she sat there, her mind reeling, she realized something horrifying: even the mightiest dragons from her stories wouldn't stand a chance against this invasion.

The alien ships released long, spindly machines that descended onto the streets like grotesque spiders. They moved with an eerie grace, scanning the wreckage with glowing red eyes. Whenever they locked onto a human, a thin beam of light followed, and within seconds, the person would vanish. No scream, no trace left behind. Just... gone.

Elowen's stomach twisted. What did they want? Why were they here?

A distant explosion shook the ground beneath them. Her father swore under his breath, grabbing the emergency radio. Static crackled.

"This is an emergency broadcast. The alien forces have taken control of major cities worldwide. Do not engage. Repeat: do not engage. Seek shelter and remain hidden. Help will come."

Help? Elowen clenched her fists. Who could possibly help against an enemy like this? They had come out of nowhere, struck with precision, and were now tightening their grip around the planet like a predator suffocating its prey.

Through the tiny gap in the curtains, she saw the aliens marching down the street. They were tall, thin, and unsettlingly smooth, as if their bodies were sculpted from liquid metal. Their heads were featureless aside from two glowing eyes that flickered like dying stars. Every movement was precise, calculated. They carried no weapons, but they didn't need any—their presence was enough to send people running.

A sharp knock at the door made her breath hitch.

Her mother grabbed her wrist, her eyes wide with terror. "Not a sound."

Another knock. Louder this time.

Elowen pressed herself against the wall, her pulse hammering in her ears. The doorknob rattled. The air was so tense she thought she might choke on it.

Then, just as suddenly as it had started, the knocking stopped. Silence stretched through the house, heavy and suffocating.

Her father let out a shaky breath, his grip on the radio tightening. "They're testing us. Seeing who's hiding."

Elowen swallowed hard. This wasn't just an attack—it was a takeover. The aliens weren't here to fight a war. They were here to claim Earth as their own. And so far, humanity had no way of stopping them.

She turned her gaze to the sketchbook on the table, filled with drawings of dragons in flight, their wings stretched wide, their fire lighting up the sky. Once, she had dreamed of a world where dragons soared above cities, powerful and free. Now, all she could think about was how much she wished those dragons were real.

Because if there was one thing Earth needed right now, it was something powerful enough to fight back.

Elowen had never known fear like this.

The night was endless, stretching on as if dawn would never come. The city was gone—its streets, its buildings, its people—reduced to broken pieces scattered across the earth. Smoke and fire twisted into the sky, and the air reeked of burning metal and something worse, something unnatural.

After a long await, it was finally dawn. The young lady took the matters into her own hands. She knew from the very bottom of her heart, that the only way to save her loved ones and the people of earth was to awaken the so called non existing creature, the Dragon.

She had no idea where to go; she followed her heart which led her to her destiny

She left her home and started a journey which she would never forget.

The Dragon Awakens

She had run for hours, slipping through the ruins, avoiding the alien patrols that hovered above the wreckage like silent vultures. The invasion wasn't over. It had only just begun.

But something else was pulling at her. A strange feeling, deep in her chest. It was like a whisper, a call from something ancient and waiting. It didn't feel like danger. It felt like... a purpose.

Her legs ached, but she kept moving, leaving the ruins behind as she sprinted into the wild, untamed forest at the city's edge. The trees stretched high above her, blocking out a very little amount of light. The deeper she went, the quieter the world became—no sirens, no explosions, just the sound of her own breath and the crunch of leaves beneath her boots.

Then she felt it.

A gust of warm air rushed past her, carrying a strange, earthy scent. The ground trembled under her feet. She stopped, her pulse hammering. The feeling in her chest grew stronger, leading her toward a jagged rock formation at the base of an enormous, ancient tree. The roots twisted around the stones like claws gripping the earth.

And in the centre—an opening.

Elowen hesitated. There was no reason to go inside. No reason at all. And yet, her feet carried her forward. The air inside was thick, heavy with something unseen. It wasn't just a cave. It was something more.

She stepped inside.

The cavern stretched far beyond what she could see, the walls lined with strange, glowing crystals. Their faint blue light flickered, casting eerie shadows along the rough stone. And then she saw them.

Nestled in a hollow of the cave, surrounded by crumbled stone and dried leaves, were **eggs.**

Not just any eggs.

They were huge, as tall as her waist, their surfaces shimmering with veins of gold, emerald, and deep crimson. They pulsed faintly, like something inside was breathing.

Elowen's chest tightened.

This wasn't possible. **It couldn't be possible.**

She had spent her entire life obsessed with dragons. Reading about them, sketching them, dreaming about them. But they weren't real. They had never been real.

Except… they were.

Because one of the eggs just **moved.**

A thin crack splintered across its surface. Then another.

Elowen stepped back, her heart hammering.

The egg shuddered. A low clicking sound filled the cave, followed by a sharp **snap.** A claw, curved and gleaming, punched through the shell. A piece crumbled away, revealing the tip of a snout—sleek, covered in damp, emerald-green scales.

Elowen couldn't breathe.

Then the whole thing **burst open.**

The baby dragon sprawled onto the cave floor, shaking bits of shell from its wings. It was stunning—its scales shimmered like polished gemstones, its tail flicked in sharp, practiced movements, and its golden eyes… **they were looking right at her.**

Elowen didn't move.

Neither did the dragon.

Then, before she could even think, the other eggs started hatching.

Cracks split the silence, shells shattered, and suddenly the cave was full of them—tiny dragons, each one different. One was deep red with black horns, another was silver with ice-blue eyes. One had wings that seemed too big for its body, another had a spiky ridge running down its back. They chirped and clicked, shaking themselves off, adjusting to the world.

Then, one of them—sleek black, with piercing silver eyes—stumbled toward her.

It sniffed the air.

Then it **trilled.** A short, sharp sound.

Elowen barely had time to process it before the emerald dragon—the first to hatch—took a step forward, too. Its head tilted, curious. Its gaze locked onto hers.

Her fingers twitched at her side. A warning voice in her head told her to step back, to be careful.

But she didn't.

She reached out.

The moment her fingertips brushed against its scales, the world **exploded.**

A searing heat shot through her, racing up her arm and into her chest. Visions slammed into her mind— **mountains engulfed in fire, a sky full of wings, ancient battles that shook the earth.**

A voice, deep and echoing, whispered in a language she didn't understand.

Then it was gone.

Elowen stumbled backward, gasping. The dragon stared at her, unblinking.

Something had just happened. Something **huge.**

And deep in her chest, she felt it.

A connection.

They knew each other now.

The Prophecy

The dragons moved closer, forming a circle around her. She could **feel** them—not just as creatures, but as something more, something woven into her very existence.

Then, out of nowhere, a voice rumbled through the cavern.

"You have awakened the last of us."

Elowen spun around, searching for the source. There was no one.

"The world falls. And only fire may rise."

The cavern trembled. The glowing veins in the walls flared brighter. The dragons' eyes burned like molten gold.

"The lost shall awaken. And you, the chosen, will either save this world…"

A deep, resounding silence filled the air.

Then—

"Or burn with it."

Elowen's stomach dropped.

This wasn't just about her.

This wasn't just about survival.

This was war.

Elowen stood at the mouth of the cavern, her heart still racing from what had just happened. The dragons—real dragons—had hatched before her very eyes, their shimmering scales reflecting the dim glow of the cave. They had bonded with her, their presence both comforting and overwhelming. She had spent the last few hours in awe, feeding them scraps from the supplies she had managed to scavenge and watching them take their first wobbly steps.

But something else had been gnawing at her—an odd sensation, like a pull in her chest. It had started the moment she had touched the dragon eggs, and now it was stronger than ever. It wasn't just her. Something—or someone—was coming.

She gripped the hilt of the small hunting knife she had kept at her side since the invasion. It wasn't much, but it was better than nothing. The dragons, sensing her unease, huddled closer.

Then, footsteps.

Not the heavy, metallic thuds of the alien machines. These were lighter, human. Someone was out there.

Elowen pressed herself against the cave wall, heart hammering. She barely breathed as a shadow approached from the entrance. Then, a figure emerged—a boy, no older than seventeen, with dirt-smeared skin and ragged clothes. His brown eyes darted around the cave before landing on her.

"You… you feel it too, don't you?" he asked, his voice hoarse from thirst.

Elowen didn't lower her knife. "Who are you?"

"My name's Kye," he said, stepping forward cautiously. "I don't know what's happening, but something—some force—brought me here. I couldn't ignore it. And… you have dragons?" His gaze flickered to the creatures behind her.

Elowen hesitated, then slowly nodded. "I do."

Kye let out a breath of disbelief, running a hand through his unkempt hair. "Then I'm not crazy. There's something bigger going on here."

Before Elowen could respond, another sound echoed through the cavern. More footsteps. She tensed again, her grip tightening on the knife.

This time, a girl stepped into view. She was tall, with dark skin and sharp, calculating eyes. Her clothes were torn, and she carried a makeshift spear—a sharpened metal rod that looked like it had been broken off from a building.

She spotted Elowen and Kye instantly. "So I'm not the only one," she muttered.

"Who are you?" Elowen asked, though she was beginning to suspect the answer.

"Liora," the girl said. "And I don't know what's going on, but I was drawn here. It was like something inside me was dragging me this way. And now I find people? And dragons?" Her eyes widened as she noticed the creatures huddled behind Elowen.

Elowen exchanged a glance with Kye. "You're not the only one. He felt it too."

Liora exhaled sharply. "Then this is no coincidence."

Before they could process what was happening, more footsteps echoed through the cavern. One by one, they arrived—seven survivors in total, each one looking just as lost and confused as the last. There was Ashan, a former medical student who had survived by hiding in the ruins of a collapsed hospital. Mira, an orphaned scavenger who had learned how to steal from the aliens without getting caught. Taron, a quiet but sharp-eyed tracker who had been surviving alone in the wilderness. And finally, Riven, a former soldier with a haunted look in his eyes, the only one among them who had real experience in combat.

Each of them had been pulled to the cave, just like Elowen. And each of them stood in stunned silence as they took in the sight of the newly hatched dragons.

"This isn't random," Kye muttered. "Something—someone—wanted us to be here."

Elowen finally stepped forward, looking at each of them. "Then maybe it's time we figure out why."

The night passed in tense discussions. The survivors shared their stories, their losses. Each of them had barely scraped by since the invasion, clinging to life in the ruins of their former world. But now, for the first time in weeks, they weren't alone.

"We need to do something," Riven said, his deep voice cutting through the silence. "We can't just hide forever. The aliens… they're getting stronger."

Mira scoffed. "And what do you suggest? Marching up to their war machines and asking them nicely to leave?"

"No," Elowen said, surprising even herself with the strength in her voice. "We fight."

Liora raised an eyebrow. "With what? A couple of dragons that can barely stand?"

"They won't stay weak forever," Elowen shot back. "They're growing. And if they really were meant to be here—to be with us—then we can train them."

Silence fell over the group as they absorbed her words.

Kye ran a hand through his hair. "You want us to build an army."

Elowen took a deep breath. "I want us to fight back."

Ashan shook his head. "This is insane."

"Is it?" Elowen stepped closer. "We were all drawn here. For what? To sit around and wait to be killed? Or to do something about it?"

The dragons stirred behind her, as if sensing her determination.

Riven leaned forward. "If we do this, there's no turning back."

"I know."

Another silence. Then, one by one, the others nodded.

Liora smirked. "Well, I always did want to ride a dragon."

A slow grin spread across Kye's face. "Then let's make history."

That night, for the first time after the invasion, they slept peacefully with their little Dragons.

As the stars flickered through the shattered sky, seven survivors and a handful of dragons made a pact.

They would fight.

And they would win.

No matter the cost.

The Gathering Storm

The next morning, Elowen didn't wait for questions.

She stood, stretching out her stiff limbs, and faced the group.

"We can't stay here forever," she said. "The aliens are still out there, and hiding won't save us. We need to fight back."

Riven scoffed. "Fight back? With what? A few knives and baby dragons?"

Elowen's jaw tightened. "We're not just survivors anymore. We're something more." She turned to the dragons, who were already growing stronger. "They were born for this. And so were we."

Liora frowned. "So you want us to be dragon riders?"

"Isn't that why we're here?" Kye added, eyes flicking between Elowen and the others. "We all felt it. That pull. Something led us here for a reason. Maybe it wasn't just to meet. Maybe it was to learn how to fight."

Mira exhaled sharply. "So we just train a dragon army overnight? Sounds easy."

"No one said it would be easy," Elowen shot back. "But we don't have a choice."

Silence settled over them. Then, slowly, Riven nodded. "Alright. If we're doing this, we do it right."

Elowen met his gaze, her heart pounding. That was all she needed to hear.

Training was brutal.

The dragons were young, their wings still learning to carry them, their fire barely more than sparks. The survivors weren't much better—half-starved, exhausted, their bodies battered by weeks of survival. But they didn't stop. They couldn't.

Elowen watched as Kye bonded with a sleek, silver dragon, its wings stretching wider every day. Liora's dragon, a deep crimson with jagged black horns, had a temper as sharp as hers. Mira, reluctant at first, found herself drawn to a quiet, observant dragon with dark blue scales that shimmered in the light.

Riven, the last to accept his role, was the first to fly. His dragon—a massive, obsidian-coloured beast with piercing gold eyes—took to the air as though it had been waiting for this moment all its life. When they landed, Riven barely spoke, but the fire in his eyes said everything.

Day by day, they became something more. Fighters. Riders. A force strong enough to challenge the monsters that had taken their world.

Then, everything went wrong.

It happened on a clear night, just as Elowen was beginning to believe they had a chance.

The ground shook. The air grew thick with the scent of burning metal.

Then—

A beam of light split the sky.

Elowen barely had time to shout before the first explosion rocked the cave, sending debris raining down around them. The dragons shrieked, their wings flaring. The others scrambled for weapons.

"Move!" Riven barked, shoving Mira out of the way as a chunk of rock slammed into the ground where she had just been standing.

Elowen spun, her heart hammering. Outside, the night was alive with movement—alien machines, their sleek metallic bodies gliding soundlessly across the sky. One of them hovered just beyond the tree line, its long, spindly limbs shifting as it scanned the area.

They had been found.

Liora grabbed her spear, eyes blazing. "We fight or we die!"

Elowen didn't hesitate. She turned to her dragon, the emerald-scaled beast that had hatched before all the others. It met her gaze and, for the first time, opened its wings.

Then they rose.

The battle was chaos. The dragons weren't ready, but neither were the aliens. The survivors fought like demons, their rage fuelled by everything they had lost. Elowen barely registered the wounds she took, her focus solely on keeping her dragon in the air, dodging the beams of searing light that carved through the sky.

Kye and Liora flanked her, their dragons darting between the towering enemy machines. Riven and Mira fought on the ground, blades flashing as they took down the smaller drones.

Then, a scream.

Elowen turned just in time to see one of the machines latch onto Ashan's dragon, its metal claws digging deep into the creature's side. Ashan cried out, trying to free it, but the alien's grip was unrelenting.

No.

Elowen didn't think. She acted.

With a scream, she dove. Her dragon folded its wings, plummeting straight toward the machine. The force of their impact sent both of them tumbling through the air, but Elowen didn't let go. She gripped the alien's cold, metallic frame and drove her knife straight into the gap between its shifting plates.

A sharp, piercing screech filled the air as the machine convulsed—then fell, crashing into the trees below.

The battle didn't end quickly. The aliens were relentless, their forces swarming. But the survivors were faster. Smarter. Stronger.

And when the last of the machines fell, the only sound left was the heavy breathing of humans and dragons alike.

Elowen staggered back, chest heaving. The night was eerily silent. They had won.

But it had been too close.

She turned to the others, their faces illuminated by the flickering remains of the fire. They were bruised, battered—but still standing.

Elowen clenched her fists.

This wasn't just a battle. It was a warning.

The aliens knew they were here.

And they would come back.

Harder.

Stronger.

But so would they.

Elowen lifted her chin. "We're not running anymore."

Kye smirked, his dragon crouching beside him. "Then what's the plan?"

Elowen met his gaze.

Elowen's words echoed through the cavern, her voice sharp with conviction. "We end this."

Silence followed, heavy with unspoken thoughts. The rebels and dragon riders exchanged looks, their faces illuminated by the flickering firelight. The weight of their mission pressed down on them, but there was something else—an unshakable determination.

They had barely begun their preparations when the warning came.

It was a low, guttural growl from one of the dragons. Ember, Elowen's companion, lifted her massive head, nostrils flaring. The other dragons shifted uneasily, their tails twitching, eyes darting toward the mouth of the cavern.

A moment later, a figure stumbled in.

A boy—thin, pale, and shaking. He looked no older than sixteen, his clothes torn, his face streaked with dirt. His chest rose and fell rapidly as he gasped for breath. When his gaze landed on Elowen, something flickered in his eyes. Hope. Desperation.

"Please," he choked out. "You have to hide. They're coming."

Elowen rushed forward, steadying him. "Who? Who's coming?"

The boy flinched as a roar sounded in the distance—not from a dragon, but from something more human. The sound of war cries, boots crunching against the earth. A moment later, torches blazed beyond the cavern entrance, casting long, menacing shadows.

And then she saw them.

A force of humans, their Armor mismatched but deadly, their weapons gleaming under the moonlight. They marched with purpose, their banners flapping in the wind. The symbol on those banners made Elowen's stomach drop.

A sword driven through a dragon's skull.

These were not allies.

These were dragon slayers.

"By the gods," whispered one of the rebels. "I thought they were all gone."

Elowen's hands curled into fists. She had heard stories of them—humans who had survived by staying hidden, not against the aliens, but against the dragons. To them, dragons weren't saviours. They were monsters. And now, they had come to finish what they started.

A booming voice rang out. "Step forward, dragon riders! Surrender the beasts, and we will let you live."

Elowen stepped forward instead, raising her chin. "We are not your enemies."

The leader of the slayers, a broad-shouldered man with a cruel scar running down his cheek, sneered. "You stand beside those things. That makes you one of them."

Ember let out a warning growl, but the slayers were unfazed. They had killed dragons before. They knew no fear.

Elowen's heart pounded. She could feel the tension in the air, the way the rebels shifted uncomfortably, some of them gripping their weapons tighter. If this turned into a fight, it would be brutal. Bloody.

And yet, she knew there was no avoiding it.

One of the slayers raised a crossbow, his aim locked onto Ember's massive chest.

Time slowed. Elowen's breath caught in her throat. The air was thick with the scent of fire and steel. Her fingers twitched toward the hilt of her blade.

The slayer fired.

Ember roared, twisting away just in time, the bolt grazing her scales. Chaos erupted.

The cavern became a battlefield. Swords clashed, arrows flew, and the cries of men and dragons alike filled the night. Elowen fought with everything she had, her blade flashing as she struck down attacker after attacker. But the slayers were relentless. They had trained for this moment.

One of them got too close, swinging an axe meant for Ember's throat. Elowen barely managed to deflect it, her arms burning with effort. The slayer snarled, driving forward again—only to be tackled by one of the rebels.

Elowen didn't have time to see who it was. Another attacker lunged, and she met him head-on, her heart hammering in her chest.

The battle was vicious, bodies locked in desperate struggle. The dragons fought too, their roars shaking the ground, flames lighting up the night. And yet, for every slayer that fell, another took their place.

They wouldn't stop. They would never stop.

Then, amidst the carnage, a chilling realization hit Elowen. The slayers weren't here just to kill. They were here to *capture*.

She turned just in time to see them dragging one of the dragons to the ground, chains wrapping around its limbs, muzzling its jaws. The dragon shrieked, thrashing, but they were prepared. More chains. More weapons. More hands forcing it down.

A sickening dread filled Elowen's chest.

They weren't just hunting dragons. They were taking them.

For what purpose, she didn't know. But she had no intention of finding out.

With a furious cry, she surged forward, striking down the slayers holding the dragon. Ember crashed into them as well, sending bodies flying. The rebels fought harder, desperation in their movements.

And finally, the tide turned.

The slayers, seeing their losses mount, began to retreat. Some ran. Others lay dead.

Only the scarred leader remained, his chest rising and falling with exertion. His gaze locked onto Elowen, burning with hatred.

"This isn't over," he hissed. "You've doomed this world."

He turned and disappeared into the darkness, leaving only the echoes of his words behind.

Elowen stood amidst the ruins of battle, her breath ragged, her body aching. The rebels and dragons stood with her, victorious but shaken.

This wasn't just a fight.

This was a warning.

A new enemy had revealed itself. And this time, they weren't outsiders. They were human.

Elowen clenched her fists, her jaw tightening.

"We end this," she said again, but this time, the meaning was different.

Not just the aliens. Not just the invasion.

But the war between humans and dragons.

Once and for all.

The silence that followed Elowen's words was heavy, the weight of their declaration settling over the camp like a storm about to break. We end this. It was more than just a call to arms—it was a promise. But as the night stretched on and the rebels rested in uneasy sleep, the wind carried whispers of a new threat.

It came just before dawn. A lone scout stumbled into camp, his face pale, his breathing ragged.

"They're coming," he gasped, collapsing to his knees. "Not the aliens. Humans. A whole faction of them—armed, trained, and they're hunting dragons."

Elowen's stomach turned. She had expected resistance, but not from their own kind.

"How many?" she demanded, already reaching for her weapons.

"Enough to wipe us out," the scout admitted grimly. "They call themselves the Dragon Slayers."

A cold dread settled over the group. They had spent years fighting to protect the dragons, risking everything to ensure their survival, and now humans—other survivors—were coming to destroy everything they had built.

Before a plan could be formed, a rustling in the trees set every warrior on edge. The dragons stirred, their keen senses detecting something unseen. Then, from the darkness, a voice rang out, steady and strong.

"You fight for monsters you do not understand."

A figure stepped into the firelight. Cloaked in a deep blue robe, his face was weathered, his eyes sharp with knowledge. He was old—far older than any of them—

but there was a presence about him, something timeless and unshaken.

Elowen's grip on her sword tightened. "And who are you?"

"I am the Keeper of the Forgotten," the man replied. "And you, child, stand at the edge of a war that began long before your kind walked this land."

The rebels exchanged wary glances, but something in the old man's voice silenced their doubts.

"The aliens are not your only enemy," he continued. "Nor are they your greatest. There is a truth buried in the past, a prophecy that speaks of this very moment. A time when dragons will rise again—not as weapons, but as the last hope for this world."

Elowen frowned. "A prophecy?"

The Keeper nodded. "Long before humans, long before the aliens, there was war. Dragons ruled the skies, but they were not alone. A force sought to control them, to twist their power for its own ends. That war never truly ended. It only lay dormant, waiting for this moment."

A shiver ran through the group. They had fought to protect the dragons, to keep them free, but they had never questioned why the aliens feared them so much.

"Then how do we stop what's coming?" Elowen asked.

"The dragons hold an ancient power, one that has been locked away for centuries. To awaken it, you must seek the lost knowledge of the First Riders." The Keeper's gaze burned into hers. "But the path will not be easy. The Dragon Slayers will not stop until the last dragon falls, and if they reach the lost knowledge before you… all will be lost."

A deep growl rumbled from one of the dragons, sensing the danger ahead.

Elowen squared her shoulders. "Then we have no choice. We find this knowledge before they do."

The Keeper gave a small nod, as if he had expected nothing less. "Then prepare yourselves, warriors of the last stand. The battle you thought you were fighting is only the beginning."

As dawn broke over the horizon, the camp burst into motion. Weapons were sharpened, supplies gathered, and dragons saddled. There was no turning back now. The real war had just begun.

The Prophecy

That night, the group slept well with a lot of hope.

As soon as it was dawn, Elowen was the first to be up. With all the weapons packed and a lot of courage, she was ready to leave for the journey.

Soon the whole group was up and all set to go. They took all they needed and the dragons who had already grown up enough to be teens.

The whole group circled. Then Elowen started her well prepared and motivating speech:

"Guys, this is the last hope for humanity. Now if we don't work together, there will be another dominant species ruling our land. We are the chosen ones who were born to protect the mother earth. This is our land and we will protect it even if we die." Shot Elowen with a voice that the group would remember forever.

The group and the dragons were never so motivated. With all their courage, they went out seeking the answers they needed.

The same force pulled them. It kept getting stronger and their heartbeat increased. They were walking like zombies which saw somebody alive.

They walked miles tirelessly as the force gave them the energy to do so. They walked and walked until they saw a cave.

"I think we have reached." Said Riven.

"Yes, the force stopped pulling us too. This is where we are supposed to be." Liora replied

They went inside.

The fire crackled in the dim cavern, casting flickering shadows on the jagged stone walls. The air was thick with tension, the only sound beyond the flames being the slow, steady breathing of the dragons resting nearby. The group sat in a loose circle, exhaustion heavy in their limbs, their minds struggling to process everything they had endured. And then, from the darkness, a voice—low, ancient, and filled with something deeper than mere wisdom.

"You seek answers," the voice rasped. "And you have come to the right place."

Elowen was on her feet in an instant, Kye and Riven mirroring her movements, their hands instinctively reaching for their weapons. The others tensed, eyes darting towards the entrance of the cave where a figure emerged from the shadows. He was old—far older than any of them had ever seen—with deep lines etched into his leathery skin, his hair a tangled mess of silver strands. His eyes, however, were clear and sharp, filled with knowledge that felt as old as the earth itself.

"Who are you?" Elowen demanded, her voice steady despite the unease curling in her chest.

The old man stepped forward, his heavy robes trailing behind him. "I am but a keeper of forgotten truths," he said. "Truths that you, Elowen, and your companions must hear."

Riven narrowed his eyes. "How do you know her name?"

A small, knowing smile touched the sage's lips. "Because the dragons know it." His gaze drifted to the slumbering creatures nearby, and at that moment, one of them—a great black-scaled beast with piercing golden eyes—lifted its head and let out a soft rumble, as if in recognition.

Elowen exchanged a glance with Kye before stepping forward. "What truths?" she asked. "Why were we drawn to this place? Why do the dragons respond to us?"

The sage gestured for them to sit. "The story begins long before human civilization," he said, his voice carrying the weight of countless years. "Before your kind built cities, before even the first written word, there was a war. A war between forces beyond your understanding. And the dragons… the dragons were not merely creatures of legend. They were warriors.”

A hush fell over the group. The dragons stirred, as if remembering.

“They were the first defenders of this world,” the sage continued. “Not against men, but against invaders. The same invaders you now face.”

Elowen’s breath caught. “You mean—the aliens?”

The old man nodded. “They came once before, long ago. But they were not victorious. The dragons, with their great power, drove them back. But such power came at a cost. The energy they wielded was too great, and it began to consume them. To protect the world, they sealed it away within their own bloodlines, locking their might into dormancy.” He paused, letting the weight of his words sink in. “Until now.”

Mira let out a slow breath. “So… what? We have dragons, but they’re weaker than they were before?”

“Not weaker,” the sage corrected. “Merely incomplete. Their true strength sleeps within them, waiting to be awakened.” His eyes met Elowen’s. “And that is why you were called.”

Elowen felt a chill run through her. “Me?”

“You and those like you.” The old man swept his gaze over the group. “Each of you carries the spark necessary to restore what was lost. But the path will not be easy. There are those who would see you fail."

A sudden sound outside the cave—metal scraping against stone. The group tensed instantly.

"Dragon slayers," Riven muttered, already reaching for his blade.

The old man didn't look surprised. "They fear what they do not understand."

Elowen's heart pounded. "And what if they get to us before we can awaken the dragons' power?"

The sage met her gaze, and for the first time, there was something else in his eyes—something that sent a shiver down her spine.

"Then," he said, "humanity will not survive this war."

A heavy silence fell. Outside, the dragon slayers were closing in. The rebels had little time, and now, more than ever, they needed to find the key to unlocking the dragons' true power. The journey ahead would be treacherous, but there was no turning back now. The prophecy had been unveiled, and the fate of the world rested in their hands.

Elowen inhaled sharply and turned to her companions. "We can't stay here. If they find us, we'll be slaughtered."

Kye nodded. "We need to move, but where?"

The old man slowly lifted his hand, gesturing toward a narrow tunnel on the far side of the cavern. "There is a path," he said. "A forgotten road that leads deep into the ancient lands. It will not be safe, but it is the only way forward."

Riven tightened his grip on his blade. "How do we know this isn't a trap?"

The old man met his gaze without flinching. "You don't. But you have no other choice."

A sound echoed from outside—the heavy clang of boots on stone. The dragon slayers were coming. The time for hesitation was over.

Elowen turned to her team. "Get the dragons ready. We leave now."

As they moved swiftly, gathering supplies and readying their mounts, the old man watched with unreadable eyes. "Remember," he said as they prepared to vanish into the darkness, "the past is not always as it seems. And the truth you seek may not be the one you wish to find."

With that cryptic warning lingering in the air, the rebels and their dragons disappeared into the unknown, the shadows of destiny closing in around them.

They jumped one by one trusting the old man blindly. They didn't have any choice either.

They had to go through dust, water, small plant that grew In the tunnel, but they didn't give up. They couldn't.

It was almost impossible to go through the tunnel with dragons, but they had to.

They came out with a jump. Their eyes left them astonished. It was an abandoned city which they saw. It was night, and the only light allowing them to see was the moonlight and some torch light strapped to each one of their head.

Their dragons moved cautiously behind them, their scaled bodies glistening under the pale moonlight. Every shadow felt like a lurking danger, every rustling leaf a warning. Something wasn't right.

Kye walked beside her, his sharp eyes scanning their surroundings. "I don't like this," he muttered under his breath. "This place is too quiet."

"I feel it too," Riven agreed, his hand gripping the hilt of his blade. "We need to be careful."

Elowen nodded, but deep down, a gnawing feeling of unease had settled in her chest. They had been following a lead—one provided by someone they trusted. The information had been too good, too precise. It was supposed to be a hidden supply cache, an untouched stockpile of weapons and food that could change the course of their fight. But now, standing amid crumbling buildings and eerie silence, she felt like they had walked into a trap.

Then, the attack came.

A blinding light exploded from the surrounding rooftops, bathing the ruins in an unnatural glow. Figures emerged from the shadows—aliens clad in sleek, obsidian Armor, their elongated limbs moving with terrifying precision. A sickening hum filled the air as their weapons powered up, the sound vibrating deep into Elowen's bones.

"Ambush!" Kye shouted, but it was already too late.

Before anyone could react, nets laced with crackling energy shot from the rooftops, ensnaring their dragons. The creatures roared in defiance, thrashing against the bindings, but the more they struggled, the tighter the nets constricted. A powerful blast struck the ground near them, sending dust and debris flying. Elowen shielded her eyes, her heart hammering in her chest.

And then she saw him.

Standing among the enemy, wearing a cold, detached expression, was Taron.

Her blood ran cold.

"No," she whispered, disbelief washing over her. "Taron? What are you doing?"

He didn't flinch. Didn't hesitate. Instead, he stepped forward, his gaze void of emotion. "I warned you," he said, his voice hollow. "Dragons are dangerous. They always have been. I made a deal—one that ensures survival."

Rage surged through Elowen. "You betrayed us," she spat. "You sold us out to them? For what? Power? A false sense of security?"

Taron's jaw tightened. "For a future," he countered. "You don't understand what you're dealing with. The aliens—they aren't just conquerors. They're something more. Something beyond us. Siding with them is the only way to survive."

Kye lunged forward, his fists clenched, but an alien soldier struck him across the face with the butt of a rifle, sending him sprawling to the ground. Before anyone could retaliate, more of the enemy swarmed in. The rebels fought back with everything they had, but they were outnumbered and outgunned. Mira darted between attackers, slashing with her twin daggers, but a pulse of energy from an alien weapon sent her crashing against a crumbling wall. Ashan tried to reach her, only to be tackled to the ground by two armoured soldiers.

Elowen swung her sword, slicing through an enemy's Armor, but for every one they took down, three more appeared. Then she felt it—a sharp pain at the back of her skull. The world spun, darkness clawing at the edges of her vision. She collapsed to her knees, the last thing she saw was Taron's expression—stone-cold, unyielding—before everything went black.

When Elowen woke, she was in a prison cell.

The walls shimmered with an eerie blue glow, humming with an unnatural energy that sent a dull ache through her skull. The air was thick with the scent of metal and something acrid, something alien. Her hands were bound in front of her, restraints glowing with the same energy as the walls.

She wasn't alone.

Kye sat in the corner, blood trickling from a cut above his eyebrow. Mira was slumped against the wall, her breathing shallow but steady. Riven paced, his muscles tense with barely restrained fury. Ashan was silent, his head bowed. They were all here—captured, broken, but alive.

Elowen clenched her fists. Taron's betrayal cut deeper than she thought possible. He had been one of them, had fought beside them, had sworn loyalty to their cause. And now, he had handed them over to their worst enemy.

A soft beeping sound filled the room, and the door slid open with a hiss.

A figure stepped inside—tall, imposing, alien. Its elongated face was devoid of emotion, its dark eyes studying them with clinical detachment. "You are resilient," it said in a voice that echoed unnaturally. "Your kind rarely survives an ambush of this scale."

Elowen forced herself to sit up straighter, meeting its gaze with defiance. "If you think we'll break, you're wrong."

The alien tilted its head. "Oh, but you will," it said smoothly. "It is only a matter of time."

Taron appeared behind the alien, his expression unreadable.

"Why?" Elowen asked, her voice raw. "After everything we've been through, after everything we've lost—why do this?"

He hesitated for the briefest moment. And in that moment, she saw something flicker in his gaze. Doubt. Regret. But it was gone as quickly as it had come. "Because I refuse to die for a losing cause."

Riven lunged forward, restrained only by his glowing cuffs. "You are a coward."

Taron didn't flinch. "I am a survivor."

Elowen's mind raced. They had to escape. The dragons were still alive—she could feel it in her very bones. And if they could get to them, if they could break free, they still had a chance.

She took a slow breath, steadying herself.

This wasn't over. Not by a long shot.

But first, they had to escape.

The prison walls were thick, made from a strange metal that pulsed faintly under the dim alien light. The air was stale, laced with the acrid scent of something unnatural. Elowen sat against the cold floor, her wrists shackled, her body aching from the ambush. The weight of betrayal pressed on her chest like a stone. They had trusted Taron. He had walked beside them, fought with them, and now, he had sold them out.

Kye sat a few feet away, his expression carved from stone. Mira had long stopped pacing, her energy drained, while Liora leaned against the wall, silent and brooding. Ashan, bruised and bloodied, tended to a wound on his arm with trembling hands. Riven, ever the soldier, was the first to break the silence. "We have to get out of here."

Elowen clenched her fists. "And how exactly do you propose we do that? We're in an alien stronghold, surrounded, and let's not forget that Taron is standing guard."

As if summoned by his name, Taron appeared outside their cell, his expression guarded, but not cruel. He wasn't gloating, wasn't laughing in their faces. If anything, he looked tired. "You don't understand," he muttered, voice barely audible. "I had no choice. If I didn't turn you in, they would have killed me."

Mira spat at the ground. "You think they won't? You think you're safe now?"

Taron exhaled sharply. "I made the only choice I could."

Elowen studied him, eyes narrowing. Taron was afraid. He had betrayed them, yes, but he was no mastermind. He was a desperate man who had chosen survival over loyalty. That fear could be used against him.

"Taron," she said, her voice soft but firm, "what if I told you that you're already dead to them?"

He flinched. "What?"

She leaned forward slightly. "You think they'll let you live? You let us escape once before, didn't you? You hesitated. And now they know you're weak. They're just waiting for a reason to kill you."

Taron swallowed hard, his gaze darting around as if expecting one of his new masters to be lurking in the shadows.

"But there's a way out," Kye added smoothly. "Let us go. Give us a chance to escape, and when we do, they'll think you died trying to stop us. You vanish. You live."

Taron hesitated. For a long moment, the only sound was the distant hum of alien machinery. Then, slowly, he reached for the key at his belt. His hands trembled as he unlocked the cell door. "You better make this look real," he whispered.

Riven didn't hesitate—he grabbed Taron by the collar and slammed him against the wall with enough force to send a resounding crash through the corridor. "That real enough for you?"

Taron gasped, clutching his ribs. "Go. Now. Before they—"

A guttural, inhuman shriek echoed down the hall. The alarm had been raised.

"Move!" Elowen barked, leading the charge.

They sprinted through the stronghold, ducking into shadowed corridors, avoiding patrolling guards as best they could. Mira grabbed a fallen alien weapon, a sleek blade that pulsed in her hands, and passed another to Liora. Ashan struggled to keep up, but Kye supported him, dragging him forward as they turned corner after corner.

Then came the gunfire.

A bolt of searing energy struck the wall beside them, leaving a molten scar. The aliens had found them.

"We need a way out!" Riven shouted, throwing himself behind cover.

Elowen's mind raced. "The docking bay! They have ships—we can steal one!"

Mira grinned. "Now that's a plan."

They barrelled forward, cutting down anything in their path. Alarms wailed, the stronghold shaking with the force of the chaos they'd unleashed. The dragons— where were the dragons? Had they been taken deeper inside? Had they—

No. She wouldn't think like that.

The docking bay loomed ahead, but a group of heavily armoured aliens stood in their path. Elowen skidded to a stop, heart pounding. They were outnumbered, outgunned.

Then, a scream. A familiar voice.

Taron.

The aliens turned their heads slightly, momentarily distracted by the sound. And in that moment, Elowen acted. She lunged, cutting one down before they had a chance to react. The others followed, a brutal clash of steel and fire erupting in the corridor.

Taron's screams continued, growing weaker. The aliens were punishing him. He had let them escape, and now he was paying the price. Elowen felt a pang of something— not sympathy, not forgiveness, but understanding. He had chosen wrong, and now he was suffering the consequences.

But she couldn't dwell on it. They reached the docking bay, hijacked a ship, and as they soared into the sky, Elowen took one last look at the stronghold below.

Somewhere in there, Taron lay broken, a man who had betrayed them for his own survival, only to be discarded like nothing.

She turned away. The war wasn't over. Not by a long shot.

Forgotten Echoes

The six survivors moved through the dense shadows of the alien spaceship, their breaths shallow, their footsteps light. The loss of their dragons weighed on them like a heavy chain, dragging behind them with every uncertain step. The world felt colder without their scaled companions, and the vast halls of the enemy's stronghold were an unforgiving reminder of what they had lost.

Elowen clenched her fists. They had escaped the clutches of their captors, but now they were lost. The ship, an immense labyrinth of strange glowing corridors and eerie humming energy, was unlike anything they had encountered before. The aliens were relentless, and without their dragons, they were vulnerable.

"We need a plan," Riven whispered, his sharp eyes darting around as they crouched behind a jagged metallic structure. "Wandering in circles is going to get us killed."

"There has to be a way out," Kye said, scanning the surroundings. "We just need to think."

Mira exhaled sharply, frustration evident in her voice. "Think? We lost everything. The dragons, our weapons—hell, even Taron sold us out before the aliens turned on him.”

“We’re not done yet,” Elowen said firmly. “We got out of that prison. We’ll find our dragons. We just have to keep moving.”

A deep silence settled over them as they pressed forward, slipping through the maze of alien corridors. It was Liora who spotted it first—a small, broken-down transport pod on the far end of a docking bay.

“That might be our way out,” she whispered.

Without hesitation, they sprinted towards it. The ship, though damaged, still hummed with power. Ashan’s fingers flew across the control panel, his medical training useless in this situation but his quick thinking invaluable. The ship sputtered to life, and with a deafening roar, they blasted out of the alien stronghold and into the vast, dark sky.

Hours later, they stood at the entrance of the same cave where it had all begun.

The cavern was silent, the remnants of their first encounter with the dragons lingering in the air like ghosts of the past. The walls, carved by time and forgotten history, whispered with unseen voices. The six of them moved cautiously, their torches casting flickering light on the damp stone.

"There must be something here," Elowen murmured, running her fingers along the jagged walls. "Something we missed."

They searched tirelessly, overturning rocks, examining every inch of the cavern. It was Kye who found it—a worn scroll hidden behind a pile of loose stones. He unrolled it carefully, the parchment fragile with age, the ink barely legible.

Elowen read aloud. "The stone of summoning… the bond unbroken. Call upon the lost, and they shall return."

Ashan furrowed his brows. "The dragons… They were meant to come to us."

Mira's eyes widened. "If this is real, then we can bring them back."

Liora was already searching. "The scroll has to be talking about something real. A stone. Something that can activate the bond."

Their hands scraped against rough rock until Riven pulled something free from the cavern's depths. A small, glowing stone, pulsing with a faint, golden light.

Elowen held it tightly, closing her eyes. She could feel something—something familiar. She focused on the bond she had once shared with her dragon, the connection that had been severed. The stone grew warmer in her grasp, vibrating with energy. Then, the cavern trembled.

A distant roar echoed through the mountains. A call.

The dragons had heard them.

It did not take long for the aliens to realize what had happened. Their monitoring systems detected the sudden surge of ancient energy. The bond between dragons and riders had been restored, and with it, a new danger had risen against them.

The six survivors had unknowingly uncovered something far more powerful than they had imagined. Not only had they called their dragons back, but the scroll also spoke of something else. Something greater.

"The dragons have powers we never knew about," Elowen whispered, reading further. "Abilities locked away, waiting to be awakened."

"The kind of abilities that could end this war," Kye added.

A sharp explosion in the distance shattered the moment. The aliens were coming.

"We have to move. Now." Riven's voice was sharp with urgency.

The six of them grabbed what little they had and ran. But this time, they weren't just running for survival.

This time, they were running toward a future where the dragons would rise again—and the war for their world would truly begin.

They give their dragons a secret touch and their wings grew larger. The dragons were now faster than the alien's spaceship.

They flew to a very distant place in a matter of seconds. Later in a secret they trained their dragons which slowly but steadily evolved.

The aliens could not catch them and nor could take their magic stone which controlled the dragons.

Hope was igniting and the chance of survival was increasing. Their dragons soon evolved big and strong dragons which left the aliens shocked.

The Ashes Of War

The night sky ignited with fire and fury. Dragons descended like living comets, their mighty wings stirring cyclones of ash and embers as they dove toward the alien stronghold. The rebels struck with everything they had.

Flames erupted across the metallic structures, turning the night into a blinding inferno. The first wave of alien sentries crumbled beneath the sheer force of the attack, their Armor melting under dragon fire.

For a moment, it seemed like victory was within their grasp.

Then the ground trembled.

From below, hidden turrets burst from the earth, their sleek designs humming with deadly energy. Before anyone could react, beams of pure light sliced through the air. One struck a dragon's wing—its agonized shriek sent a chill through Elowen's bones.

"Kye, MOVE!" she shouted, just as another beam seared the air where he had been moments before.

He twisted his body, barely avoiding the blast, his dragon roaring in pain as its side was grazed. Smoke filled his lungs, but he forced himself to stay focused.

"The shields!" Mira's voice cut through the chaos. "They have shielding over the stronghold!"

As if in response, shimmering blue barriers flickered into existence, encasing the structures. The alien defences had been waiting for them.

From the darkness, a squad of cybernetically enhanced warriors charged forward. Their movements were unnatural—swift, calculated, merciless. One moment, Liora was slashing through the battlefield; the next, she was yanked from her dragon's saddle, disappearing into the shadows.

"Liora!" Riven's desperate shout was swallowed by the chaos. He wheeled his dragon around, but the battle was too thick. He couldn't reach her.

"We need to breach the shields!" Elowen called, slicing down an alien that lunged for her. "Find a weak point!"

Mira's sharp eyes darted over the field. Then she saw it— a pulse, just beneath the central tower. A point where the shield fluctuated for a fraction of a second. It was small, but it was there.

"There!" she pointed. "Hit it with dragon fire! Now!"

The dragons unleashed torrents of flame, striking at the exact moment the pulse flickered. The energy field wavered, then shattered apart in a violent explosion.

Ashan surged forward through the breach, his dragon barrelling past enemy lines. But as soon as they broke through, a new nightmare awaited them.

A monstrous alien beast stepped from the shadows, towering over the battlefield. Four arms, each wielding a humming energy blade, its eyes glowing with intelligence and cruelty.

Ashan skidded to a stop.

"Oh, that's not fair."

The creature moved impossibly fast. One blade cut through the air, forcing Ashan to duck just in time. His dragon roared, its talons swiping at the enemy, but the creature dodged every attack as if it knew them before they happened.

Then the ground trembled again.

Before anyone could react, a deafening CRACK split the air. The battlefield collapsed beneath them. The rebels plunged into darkness, swallowed by the earth itself.

Elowen hit the ground hard. Dust filled her lungs as she struggled to breathe. The air smelled of damp stone and something ancient.

A groan echoed in the cavern. Kye pushed himself up beside her, coughing. "Where... are we?"

Elowen lifted her gaze. The cavern walls pulsed with an eerie glow, illuminating rows upon rows of dragon eggs, their surfaces smooth and untouched by time.

Her heart clenched.

This wasn't just a cave. It was a tomb of forgotten dragons.

Above, the battle raged on. Riven fought to hold the line, but the aliens were closing in. And as Elowen's eyes adjusted to the dim light, she realized they weren't alone.

A figure emerged from the shadows.

Her blood ran cold.

It was someone she knew. Someone she thought had perished long ago.

"Elowen," the figure said, voice laced with cruel amusement. "It's been a long time."

The world tilted. She couldn't breathe.

This war had just become personal.

Meanwhile, Ashan knew they were losing. He had one chance left—a hidden power within the dragons, locked away for centuries. A desperate gamble.

He closed his eyes. Focused.

The air around his dragon shifted, the temperature spiking. A deep, guttural growl rumbled from the beast's throat. Then—

A blinding explosion of light erupted.

The battlefield fell silent.

Then, all hell broke loose.

The aliens then fled. Nobody died, but all of them were injured and not ready for any further attacks.

The battle was over, but the cost was immeasurable. The battlefield smouldered under a dying sun, the scent of charred metal and scorched earth lingering in the air. Elowen stood amidst the wreckage, her heart pounding in her chest as she surveyed what remained of their rebellion. They had won, but only barely. The cost of victory was painted in the blood and ash that coated their skin.

Kye clutched his wounded shoulder, grimacing as Mira helped him onto his feet. Ashan's dragon lay panting, one of its wings torn, while Riven limped toward them, his face set in a grim scowl. Liora was silent, her gaze lost in the distance. They had fought harder than ever before, and yet survival felt like an illusion slipping through their fingers.

"We can't stay here," Riven said, voice tight. "The aliens will regroup. They always do."

Elowen exhaled sharply, glancing at their injured dragons. They needed rest, but rest meant death if the aliens returned. They had to move. Now.

"There's a place," she said, forcing the words through exhaustion. "A hidden cache. Food, weapons, supplies. A stronghold that was abandoned before the war began. If we can reach it…"

Mira nodded. "Then we stand a chance."

A chance was all they had.

The journey was brutal. They rode hard through the ravaged wasteland, pushing their battered bodies and exhausted dragons beyond their limits. Each step felt heavier, as though the weight of the battle dragged them further into the earth. The alien patrols were everywhere—watching, waiting.

They avoided the open roads, cutting through dense forests and jagged ravines. Every rustle in the trees sent their hands to their weapons. Every distant hum of an alien ship overhead forced them into the shadows. They were prey, hunted by an enemy that never rested.

By the third day, the dragons could barely walk. Kye nearly collapsed from dehydration, and Mira's fingers trembled from exhaustion as she tended to the wounded. But the stronghold was close now. Just beyond the next ridge.

"We're almost there," Elowen whispered, though she didn't know if it was for them or herself.

They crested the hill, and there it was—an old underground facility, half-buried beneath layers of rubble. Its metal doors stood rusted but intact, hidden by overgrown vines and twisted roots. It had been untouched for years.

"Come on," Riven urged. "Before they find us."

With the last of their strength, they pushed forward.

Inside, the air was stale, thick with dust and time. But it was safe. Supplies lined the walls—ancient weapons, preserved rations, medical kits. A chance at survival. A chance to fight another day.

Kye sank against the wall, his breath coming in ragged gasps. "I never… want to move again."

Mira chuckled weakly, sliding down beside him. "Agreed."

Elowen closed her eyes, exhaustion threatening to pull her under. They had made it. They had survived. But as her fingers traced the edge of an old map pinned to the wall, a cold dread settled over her.

Something was missing.

Then she heard it.

A distant, inhuman screech.

Her blood turned to ice.

"They found us," she whispered.

Outside, the night lit up with the glow of alien warships. The ground trembled beneath their feet. The battle wasn't over.

But none of them had the stamina to fight, so they just fled to a place very far away. They eat and fed their dragons. Their health was restored and they were ready for training and to win the war.

The Revealing Twist

With the health restored, the seven but now six survivors were again off in the air exploring. They had an idea; they would go to the enemy and spy on them. They left for the journey.

The journey through the wastelands was gruelling. Every step forward felt like a battle against the weight of exhaustion, despair, and the unknown. The rebels had endured countless hardships, pushing past their limits with the singular goal of reclaiming their world. The air was thick with the scent of burnt earth, the remnants of past battles staining the sky with an eerie haze. Silence hung heavy around them, broken only by the rustling of wings and the distant echo of something unnatural—something waiting in the shadows.

Elowen rode at the front, her emerald-scaled dragon beneath her, moving with a quiet grace that belied the tension in the air. The other dragons soared above, their powerful forms slicing through the sky, watchful and ready. The survivors rode in tight formation, their eyes weary yet burning with determination. Kye, Riven, and the others exchanged brief glances but spoke little. Words had become unnecessary; the battle they had fought so far had forged an unbreakable bond between them.

As they neared the alien stronghold—a towering, pulsating structure that seemed almost alive—unease settled in Elowen's chest like a stone. Something was wrong. The dragons, usually attuned to their riders, began shifting uneasily, their movements more hesitant, their eyes flickering with an emotion she couldn't quite place. Then, before anyone could react, a deep, resonant sound rippled through the air. It was not loud, but it vibrated through the bones, through the very soul.

And that was when the dragons turned.

One by one, as if summoned by an unseen force, the dragons veered away from their riders. Some screeched in protest, others struggled as if caught between two commands—but the pull was too strong. Wings beat against the wind, tails lashed, and the once-loyal beasts abandoned their companions, heading straight toward the stronghold. Panic erupted among the rebels.

"No! Come back!" Mira's voice cracked with disbelief as her dragon—a beast she had raised from an egg— soared away without hesitation. Kye cursed, reaching out futilely as his own mount left him behind. The rebels fell into chaos, their strongest allies now part of the enemy's ranks.

But not all.

Two dragons remained.

Elowen's emerald-scaled companion stood firm, golden eyes flickering with conflict but refusing to leave. Riven's midnight-blue dragon, scarred from battle and loyal to the core, planted its feet on the ground, its nostrils flaring in defiance.

The realization hit like a punch to the gut—while the others had succumbed, these two had not. Their bond with their riders ran deeper than whatever command had called the others away.

"Elowen…" Riven's voice was tight, barely above a whisper. "What the hell is happening?"

Elowen didn't have an answer. Her hands clenched the reins as she watched the remaining dragons vanish beyond the alien gates, her heart a storm of rage and betrayal. How could this be? They had fought side by side, lived and bled together—and now they had turned?

Then the truth struck.

The dragons were never meant to be humanity's salvation.

The realization left her breathless. The aliens had not just invaded; they had orchestrated everything. The dragons had not been Earth's defenders. They had been weapons, waiting to be activated. The prophecy that had guided them, the hope that had kept them fighting—it had all been a carefully laid deception. The dragons' power had never been meant for them.

Kye's expression twisted with fury. "This was never a war for survival… it was a war for control. And we've been playing into their hands this whole time."

The weight of betrayal settled over them like a suffocating fog. Elowen could see it in the others' eyes—Mira's silent devastation, Ashan's clenched fists, Liora's trembling breath. They had risked everything, only to find that their greatest allies had been the enemy's pawns all along.

A heavy stillness settled as they stared at the stronghold. The sky above it pulsed with an unnatural glow, as if the very air trembled with anticipation. They were running out of time.

The weight of betrayal hung heavy over them. The realization that their dragons had answered the call of the enemy cut deeper than any wound. They had fought, bled, and trusted—only to watch their own allies turn against them. The rebels sat in silence, their camp reduced to nothing but flickering embers and broken spirits. Even the two dragons who had refused to follow the call—Riven's midnight-scaled beast and Mira's silver-winged companion—lay low, sensing the despair thick in the air.

Kye was the first to break the silence. He stood, his jaw clenched, fire in his eyes. "We're not done yet. We still have warriors, and more importantly, we have knowledge. We know how these creatures think, how they move. If they want a war, we'll give them one they'll never forget. We use guerilla warfare. We strike fast, we vanish. We use every inch of this land to our advantage."

A murmur spread through the group. It wasn't just mindless hope—there was a strategy in his words. Riven nodded slowly, his usual scepticism tempered by the fire of purpose. "We have dragon slayers among us," he added. "People who've spent their whole lives hunting and fighting dragons. They might hate what dragons have done, but they hate the aliens more. If we convince them, we turn their skills into our advantage."

Elowen exhaled, her mind racing. "And we don't just fight—we build an army. We rescue those still fighting to survive. The aliens think humanity is broken, scattered. Let's prove them wrong. We bring them together."

A spark of hope flickered among the group. This wasn't over.

The plan formed quickly. Two of their own—Liora and Ashan—would head out to find the dragon slayers, to show them the truth and convince them to join forces. If they succeeded, they would gain some of the deadliest fighters against dragons—fighters now turned against the very creatures the aliens sought to control.

Meanwhile, Riven and Mira would take their dragons, the only two who had stayed by their side, and search for human survivors. They would move silently, deep into the ruins of cities, finding those willing to fight, those who had been waiting for a spark to reignite their will to resist. They would not come back alone.

And finally, Elowen and Kye would do what no one else would dare—break into an alien stronghold. The weapons of humanity had proven almost useless against the invaders' advanced technology, but if they could steal from the enemy itself, they could change the course of the war. It was the most dangerous mission, but also the most vital.

They spent the night preparing. They gathered supplies, whispered final words of encouragement, and hardened their hearts for what was to come. As the first light of dawn painted the horizon in muted gold, Elowen stood before them all.

"We were broken, but we are not defeated. We were betrayed, but we are not weak. They think they have won. Let's prove them wrong. Let's show them that humanity does not surrender. We rise. We fight. We take back what's ours."

A roar of agreement filled the air. This was not the sound of the defeated—this was the sound of warriors. Of rebels ready to reclaim their world.

And as they set off, each on their own path, the war had already begun.

The War Begins

The night before the battle, the survivors sat together beneath the vast, endless sky, the stars twinkling like silent witnesses to their fragile hopes. The fire crackled between them, casting soft, flickering shadows over their faces, filling the air with the comforting scent of burning wood. There was no Armor, no weapons in their hands—just them, sitting close, sharing stories, laughter, and quiet dreams of what life would be like after they won.

Riven leaned back against a smooth rock, exhaling as he looked up. "You ever think about what you'll do when this is over?" he asked, his voice quieter than usual.

Mira smiled softly, tracing patterns in the dirt. "I'd like to rebuild the town where I grew up. Maybe even start teaching kids how to fight so they'll never have to live in fear again."

Liora laughed. "That suits you. Always planning for the next fight."

Ashan nodded. "We'll need people like you. Warriors who don't just fight for survival, but for something bigger."

Kye poked at the fire with a stick, his expression unreadable. "If we make it through this… I'd like to find a place where people and dragons can truly live side by side. No fear, no war. Just… peace."

Elowen's heart ached at the thought. How beautiful that sounded. How impossible it seemed. But in this moment, with her friends around her, it felt real—like a future she could almost reach out and touch.

The conversation grew quieter as the night stretched on. The fire dwindled to embers, the warmth of companionship keeping them close. For the first time in what felt like forever, they let themselves be human. They spoke about their families, their pasts, and the little things they missed—freshly baked bread, the sound of rain against a window, the smell of home.

There was a lingering warmth between them all, a closeness that went beyond friendship. In another world, in another time, this might have been something more. Something deeper. But as Mira tilted her head toward Ashan, as if to say something meaningful, he let out a short breath and brushed it off with a chuckle. "Come on, we should get some rest. Big day tomorrow."

Reality settled in again. The warmth remained, but the dream of something more faded like smoke into the air.

The sun had not yet risen, but the air was thick with tension. In the hidden base deep within the ruined valley, the rebels gathered in a circle, their faces illuminated by the flickering fire at the centre. The weight of the moment pressed upon them all, heavier than any battle they had faced before. They knew what lay ahead. They knew the odds. Yet, in this moment, they needed something beyond strategy—something to remind them why they fought.

Kye stepped forward, his presence commanding yet solemn. He let his gaze drift over each warrior, each survivor who had endured unimaginable loss. His voice, when it finally came, was steady and strong, cutting through the heavy silence like steel through flesh.

"We stand here today not as victims of fate, but as its defiers," Kye began, his voice echoing against the cold walls of the cavern. "The aliens thought they could break us. They took our homes, our families, our dragons. They burned our cities, slaughtered our people, and left us to die in the ashes. But look at us. We are still here. We are not broken. We are not defeated."

Murmurs of agreement rippled through the crowd. Some clenched their fists. Others bowed their heads in quiet reverence.

Kye took a breath and stepped closer to the fire. "This is not just a fight for survival. This is a fight for every human who was stolen from this world. Every dragon who was forced into servitude. Every child who was robbed of a future. We do not fight because we wish to. We fight because if we do not, no one else will. And I swear to you, no matter what happens out there, we will give them a war they will never forget."

A roar of agreement rose from the rebels, the sound of defiance filling the cavern. They had suffered. They had bled. But today, they would strike back.

Dawn broke as they reached the battlefield. The valley stretched before them, its open plains soon to be stained with blood. Their trap was set—hidden trenches lined with sharpened spikes, archers concealed among the trees, and their strongest fighters waiting just beyond sight, prepared to strike the moment the aliens crossed into their killing ground.

Mira climbed onto a broken stone pillar, her figure casting a long shadow as she turned to face the assembled warriors. The dragon slayers stood among them now, their distrust put aside for this final stand. The remaining free humans, those they had rescued, stood armed and ready. And at the heart of it all stood the last of the true dragon riders, Elowen and the few dragons that had remained loyal.

Mira's voice was fierce as she addressed them. "Our plan is simple, but it must be executed with precision. The moment the aliens reach the centre of the valley; we unleash our arrows. They will not expect it. The moment they look up, we strike from below. And when they realize they are trapped, our hidden force will strike from behind. Today, we do not fight for revenge. We fight for the future. For every life taken, we will take theirs. For every home destroyed, we will make them bleed. We will not fall today, because we cannot afford to!"

The roar that followed was deafening. They were ready. They had to be.

The aliens arrived in the valley, their ranks stretching wide. Their monstrous forms gleamed in the sunlight, towering creatures of steel and flesh. The enslaved dragons flew overhead, shadows passing over the battlefield like a dark omen. The moment they stepped into the heart of the valley, Mira raised her hand.

"NOW!"

The sky darkened as a storm of arrows rained down, striking the aliens with deadly precision. The creatures roared in agony as the projectiles pierced their Armor. Those that charged forward found themselves swallowed by the hidden trenches, impaled by spikes before they could react.

And then, from the trees, the second force attacked. The dragon slayers, armed with their enchanted weapons, struck down the enslaved dragons with swift precision. The ground shook with the force of the battle, blood staining the grass as the rebels fought with everything they had.

It was working. The aliens were being driven back. They were winning.

Until they weren't.

A single shot rang out. A flare, fired from behind enemy lines. And in that moment, the rebels knew. They had been betrayed.

The hidden army that had been striking from behind suddenly found themselves ambushed. The dragons they thought were downed roared back to life, their wounds fake, their loyalty to the aliens never severed. The aliens had known their plan all along.

The battle turned into a massacre.

One by one, the rebels fell. Mira fought until the very end, her sword clashing against the enemy's steel, but she was overrun. Ashan's screams echoed through the valley before they were silenced. Riven stood his ground, defiant until his last breath, but even he could not hold back the tide. The dragon slayers, the humans, every last one of them—gone.

Kye was the last to fall. His body broken, his breath ragged, he turned to Elowen, his voice barely a whisper. "Run. Live. Make it mean something."

And then he was gone.

Elowen stood in the centre of the battlefield, her emerald dragon the only thing left beside her. Blood soaked the ground. The bodies of her friends lay scattered like broken dolls. The weight of their sacrifice crushed her, an unbearable sorrow that settled deep within her bones.

She had failed. They had all failed.

Everything Gone

The wind howled through the ruins of the battlefield, carrying the scent of blood and ash. The fires had long since died down, leaving only smouldering embers in the remnants of a war that should have been their victory. Elowen stood alone amidst the destruction, her emerald dragon—her only remaining companion—resting silently behind her. Everything was gone. Everyone was gone.

She tried to move, but her body refused. The weight of grief pinned her down, pressing into her chest like an iron hand. Her fingers curled into the dirt, trembling. The battlefield stretched around her, littered with the bodies of her friends, of those who had fought beside her, believed in her. Kye's voice echoed in her mind—the way he had laughed, the fire in his eyes when he had spoken of freedom. Gone. Mira, Ashan, Riven. Their faces blurred together, slipping through her mind like sand between her fingers. She had failed them.

Her mind drifted back to a time before the war, before the chaos. Her home had been warm then, filled with laughter. She could still hear the crackling of the hearth, smell the sweet scent of freshly baked bread. She could see her mother smiling at her across the table, her father's hand ruffling her hair, her younger brother tugging at her sleeve, begging her to tell him stories of the dragons. And her friends—Kye teasing her as they raced through the fields, Mira braiding her hair as they spoke of a future filled with dreams. Those moments felt like a different life. A cruel memory left to haunt her.

She squeezed her eyes shut, trying to block it out, but the images played relentlessly. The warmth of those days was a ghost now, and she was its last lingering echo. What was left for her in this world? No home, no family, no friends. Only the crushing weight of loss and the unbearable silence of survival.

The dragon beside her let out a soft rumble, pressing its nose against her shoulder. She didn't react. Even her companion's presence felt distant, like a shadow of what once was. She had nothing left. No fight, no vengeance, no will. What was she supposed to do? Rebuild? Start again? How could she when every step forward would be a reminder of those who were missing?

The sky above was endless, stretching over the broken land. The stars blinked down at her, indifferent to the suffering below. Once, she had looked up at them with hope, dreaming of the future she would create. Now, they felt cold and unreachable, like every dream she had ever held.

She exhaled shakily, her breath visible in the cold night air. One step. Then another. Her feet carried her forward, away from the battlefield, away from the wreckage of her past. There was no destination, no goal. She walked simply because standing still would mean being consumed by the void within her. The dragon followed, silent as a shadow.

The forest swallowed her whole, the darkness pressing in on all sides. The trees whispered with the wind, their branches creaking like voices speaking of forgotten things. She didn't care where she was going. She didn't care if she never returned. The world had taken everything from her—her home, her people, her heart. And so, she gave it the only thing left to give.

Herself.

And with that, she disappeared into the night, never to be seen again.

TO BE

CONTINUED...

www.ingramcontent.com/pod-product-compliance
Lightning Source LLC
Chambersburg PA
CBHW022055150726
47990CB00003B/1093